George Feydeau's

The Lady
From Maxim's

Adapted by Gene Feist

Based on a literal translation by
Catherin M. Perebinossoff and Mierre

A SAMUEL FRENCH ACTING EDITION

SAMUEL
FRENCH

FOUNDED 1830

New York Hollywood London Toronto

SAMUELFRENCH.COM

MUSIC

Music for this production is available on a rental and deposit basis.

Royalty for use of the music is $10.00 for each performance. We can lend you a piano score of the music, for a period of eight weeks, on receipt of the following:

1. Number of performances and exact performance dates.

2. Royalty in full on the music for the entire production.

3. Deposit of $10.00, which is refunded on return of the material in good condition immediately after your production. Plus first-class postage and handling charge of 75¢ for the piano score.

THE LADY FROM MAXIM'S was given its American Premiere by the Roundabout Theatre Co., Inc., on May 3, 1970, with the following cast:

DR. LUCIEN PETIPON .... *Brian Hartigan*

GABRIELLE .... *Gloria Starita*

ETIENNE .... *Edwin Lewis*

DR. MONGICOURT .... *Sterling Jensen*

GENERAL .... *Norman Lind*

CORIGNON .... *Charles Anatra*

LADY .... *Marsha Katzakian*

DUKE OF VALMONTE .... *Philip Campanella*

STREET CLEANER .... *Robert McCrary*

VILLAGE PRIEST .... *Anthony De Vito*

BROTHER JULIAN .... *Tony Zanetta*

CLEMENTINE .... *Jennifer Boyd*

SIMONE .... *Yvonne Patterson*

Directed by *Gordon Heath*
Sets by *Lorna Hainesworth*
Costumes by *Mimi Maxmen*
Incidental Music by *Philip Campanella*

CAST

DR. LUCIEN PETIPON, *a surgeon*

GABRIELLE, *his wife*

ETIENNE, *his servant*

DR. MONGICOURT, *his associate*

GEN. PETIPON, *his uncle*

CLEMENTINE, *General's ward*

LT. CORIGNON, *her fiancé*

SIMONE, *her companion*

THE LADY, *a cocotte*

DUKE OF VALMONTE

A STREET CLEANER

VILLAGE PRIEST

BROTHER JULIAN

TIME: Spring, the turn of the century

PLACE: Paris, Dr. Petipon's study and at Touraine, the garden of General Petipon's chateau

The Lady from Maxim's

ACT ONE

The drawing room of Dr. Petipon. r. *is a portion of the
Doctor's bedroom. As the Act begins, the stage is
dark and the voices of* Dr. Mongicourt *and the
servant* Etienne *are heard offstage* d. r.

Mongicourt. Good morning, Etienne.
Etienne. Good morning, monsieur.
Mongicourt. Your master up and about?
Etienne. No, monsieur.

(*They enter.*)

Mongicourt. You are right, Etienne.
Etienne. That is my fate, monsieur.
Mongicourt. Your fate?
Etienne. To always be right in a world that does not
appreciate perfection.
Mongicourt. Oh, if we physicians could only have
your sublime confidence.
Etienne. Impossible—you would never be willing to
serve those years of apprenticeship. It is no easy thing to
be a perfect servant—
Mongicourt. And what can the perfect servant tell us
about his master?
Etienne. Dr. Petipon sleeps. At 8 A.M. winter, spring,
summer, and fall Dr. Petipon rises for a cold bath—
Mongicourt. And?
Etienne. It is noon—and he sleeps— Monsieur? Is
this the end of the world?

MONGICOURT. Perhaps the end of one way of life and the beginning of another.

ETIENNE. I would not like that, monsieur. I would not like to see my years of training go to waste.

MONGICOURT. Years of training?

ETIENNE. Dr. Petipon was most cooperative but it took a great deal of effort to introduce him to steady habits. And to think he drinks nothing stronger than mineral water.

MONGICOURT. I fear, Etienne, something stronger than mineral water has been at work.

ETIENNE. Perhaps you are in the need of an extraordinarily competent servant, sir?

MONGICOURT. Desertion for just one transgression?

ETIENNE. Perhaps I am a bit too harsh.

MONGICOURT. I think so, Etienne.

ETIENNE. I want to thank you, monsieur, for reminding me of my duty.

MONGICOURT. That's one of my specialties, advice.

ETIENNE. Unsolicited.

MONGICOURT. No charge. Do you think we might awaken the good doctor?

ETIENNE. Have you a loaded pistol?

MONGICOURT. Pistol?

ETIENNE. Chinese firecracker?

MONGICOURT. Firecracker?

ETIENNE. Or a brass gong?

MONGICOURT. Brass gong?

ETIENNE. In short, monsieur, there is no way to awaken Dr. Petipon except perhaps gunfire—

MONGICOURT. The man sleeps soundly? (*In.*)

ETIENNE. Like the dead!

MONGICOURT. But I can't stay here indefinitely.

ETIENNE. Can you sing?

MONGICOURT. Can I sing?

ETIENNE. If you can sing—he does respond to music. Why, I don't know—since he is quite tone deaf.

MONGICOURT. If you think it will be of any help.

(*Warms up. Assails a musical scale. Starts "Frère Jacques."*)

SONG: "ARE YOU SLEEPING?"
(*Music of "Frère Jacques."*)

Are you sleeping,
Are you sleeping,
(M'sieur) Petipon?
(M'sieur) Petipon?
   Time you should be stirring.
   Time you should be stirring.
   It's past noon,
   It's past noon.

(ETIENNE *claps for* MONGICOURT, *gets progressively angrier.*)

ETIENNE. We shall proceed with our limited facilities. Follow me. (MONGICOURT *literally follows* ETIENNE *across the room to face the Doctor's sleeping alcove.*) Monsieur? Monsieur? Where are you, monsieur? (MONGICOURT *has kept behind* ETIENNE *who does not discover him until he speaks up.*)
   MONGICOURT. I've followed you.
   ETIENNE. I meant musically.

(ETIENNE *proceeds to sing and after a few measures is joined by* MONGICOURT. *They sing together loudly and lustily until* MONGICOURT *suddenly stops.*)

MONGICOURT. What was that?
ETIENNE. Monsieur?
MONGICOURT. The cry of a wounded animal?
ETIENNE. Success!
MONGICOURT. Success?
ETIENNE. It's my master, Dr. Petipon; he is beginning to stir.

MONGICOURT. Petipon. It is I . . . It is me . . . It is we . . . It is Mongicourt. . . .

PETIPON. (*Moans and groans.*) Who?

MONGICOURT. Mongicourt, your dear friend.

PETIPON. No, the other one.

MONGICOURT. Petipon?

PETIPON. Is that my name?

ETIENNE. Monsieur—you are Dr. Petipon.

PETIPON. Who is speaking?

ETIENNE. Etienne, your loyal, faithful and true servant.

PETIPON. The name has a familiar ring.

MONGICOURT. Etienne?

PETIPON. The other one. What name did you say?

MONGICOURT. Petipon!

PETIPON. That's my name.

MONGICOURT. (*To* ETIENNE.) I'd swear . . .

ETIENNE. Where are you, Dr. Petipon?

MONGICOURT. (*Howls.*) Ooh hoo!

PETIPON. Here in my bed.

MONGICOURT. (*He and* ETIENNE *move a small sofa and look down at* PETIPON *who has been sleeping blissfully beneath it.*) Come, Petipon, get up from there.

PETIPON. Nothing will budge me from my bed.

MONGICOURT. But you are not in your bed.

PETIPON. Not in my bed? Not in my bed? Where am I if not in my bed?

ETIENNE. Dr. Petipon—you have been sleeping on the floor.

PETIPON. I didn't ask your opinion. What time is it?

ETIENNE. Shortly after noon.

PETIPON. You mean midnight.

MONGICOURT. He means noon.

PETIPON. If it is noon why is it black out?

MONGICOURT. Open your eyes.

PETIPON. I'm afraid.

MONGICOURT. I'll hold your hand.

PETIPON. I'll be brave. (*Horrible shriek.*) It's true. It is daylight and I've been poisoned.

ETIENNE. I told you monsieur wasn't drunk.

PETIPON. I, drunk! Could alcohol be responsible for a—a blinding headache, b—a swollen tongue, c—vague but alarming sensations in the lower abdomen? (*Groan.*)

MONGICOURT. That's right.

PETIPON. I know it's right but I still feel as sick as a dog.

ETIENNE. Would you like some food?

PETIPON. Are you mocking me?

ETIENNE. I?

PETIPON. You!

ETIENNE. No, monsieur.

PETIPON. No what?

ETIENNE. I am not mocking you.

PETIPON. Get out, get out, get out!

ETIENNE. (*Starts to exit.*) Very well, monsieur.

PETIPON. Stop!

ETIENNE. Yes, monsieur?

PETIPON. Where is my wife, Gabrielle?

ETIENNE. She has taken a hand-embroidered prayer stole to the Vicar of St. Sulpice.

MONGICOURT. Your wife is devout?

PETIPON. Fanatically.

ETIENNE. She's had visions and visitations.

MONGICOURT. Is this true?

PETIPON. Two days in a row. Only last month—she looked at me and saw the Virgin.

ETIENNE. In blue veils. . . .

PETIPON. Most disconcerting.

ETIENNE. She can also speak to the departed.

PETIPON. Who, the Virgin?

ETIENNE. Madame.

PETIPON. Get out—get out—get out.

ETIENNE. I take my leave, monsieur. (*He exits* D. R.)

PETIPON. There are times when I suspect that that man is impertinent.

MONGICOURT. Why do you hold your head?

PETIPON. To keep it from falling off.

MONGICOURT. Your voice indicates that you somehow blame me.

PETIPON. And with good cause.

MONGICOURT. You wrong me.

PETIPON. Who has played the serpent in my garden of Eden?

MONGICOURT. You're not referring to me—?

PETIPON. I am.

MONGICOURT. But that is absurd.

PETIPON. You deny any implication? You wash your hands of the matter?

MONGICOURT. That's right. . . . We were washing our hands. I said to you—"Petipon," I said. "Petipon, we have just completed an intricate, oh, so delicate operation. Let's sew up the poor devil's stomach and go have a drink." That's all I said.

PETIPON. And where did you take me? Where did he take me? Maxim's—Maxim's.

MONGICOURT. Surely five minutes at Maxim's does not justify this personal and unwarranted attack upon me?

PETIPON. It's what those five minutes led to . . ₂ ! Five minutes!

MONGICOURT. I am not my brother's keeper.

PETIPON. But you could have been your professional associate's keeper.

MONGICOURT. Just how long did you stay on after I left?

PETIPON. You dare ask?

MONGICOURT. I'm curious. How late did you stay?

PETIPON. It's all like a horrible dream—I remember nothing.

MONGICOURT. Ah. When you did not report this morning to the clinic I made your rounds. I saw all of your patients.

PETIPON. My client in surgery?

MONGICOURT. Resting comfortably.

PETIPON. No pain?

MONGICOURT. None.

PETIPON. And the operation?

MONGICOURT. Splendid achievement. Your skill and dexterity would have pleased him. Too bad he died last night.

(MADAME PETIPON'S *voice is heard offstage.*)

MADAME PETIPON. Etienne! Oh dear, oh dear, oh dear!

ETIENNE. Yes, madame.

MADAME PETIFON. Has my husband awakened?

ETIENNE. More or less, madame.

PETIPON. What does he mean by that? How do I look?

MONGICOURT. Dreadful.

(MADAME PETIPON *enters* D. R.)

MADAME PETIPON. Ah, there you are. Up and about— How do you do, Doctor Mongicourt?

MONGICOURT. I feel dreadful.

MADAME PETIPON. (*To* PETIPON.) On closer viewing— you don't look at all well, my dear. My poor darling, what is it?

MONGICOURT. Have no fear, madame. I have been discussing Dr. Petipon's condition and it is nothing more than a mild case of Maxima Maxima.

MADAME PETIPON. Maxima?

MONGICOURT. Maxima Maxima, nothing infectious. Nothing to be alarmed about. Bed rest, spirits of ammonia, aspirin. In a day or two he'll be his old self, only, of course, a bit older.

MADAME PETIPON. Strange—you didn't feel at all feverish when I kissed you this morning.

PETIPON. Kissed me? Where?

MADAME PETIPON. In your Turkish corner. You were wrapped up in the blankets like a wild Indian. Only after great effort did I discover a bit of forehead on which to press my lips. At that moment as I have testified—he was quite cool. Why did you start?

PETIPON. I did not start—I am pleased. Yes, pleased—quite pleased. (*Insists.*)

MADAME PETIPON. You need an herbal tea to settle your nerves and your stomach.

MONGICOURT. An excellent prescription. It constantly amazes me how instinctively alert to medical disciplines—doctors' wives are.

MADAME PETIPON. Ah, my herbal teas are celebrated in the parish. Now don't overdo, my dear Lucien. Come, Etienne.

PETIPON. (*Sits chaise L.*) Ooh! She kissed my forehead.

MONGICOURT. She said.

PETIPON. In my bed!

MONGICOURT. She said.

PETIPON. I slept there. Don't you understand? I am a sleepwalker.

MONGICOURT. A sleepwalker?

PETIPON. I remember absolutely nothing. (*A sneeze is heard from the alcove. To* MONGICOURT:) Is that all you can say?

MONGICOURT. I said nothing. (*Another sneeze is heard.*)

PETIPON. You insist you said nothing?

MONGICOURT. That was a sneeze!

PETIPON. Ah!

MONGICOURT. But it was not I who sneezed.

PETIPON. Oh?

MONGICOURT. It was not you who sneezed.

PETIPON. Dear friend—you are trying to tell me something. Speak! In the name of God speak!

LADY. (*Sits up in the alcove bed.*) What would you like me to say? (*Is wearing a slip and is wrapped in a bed sheet.*)

PETIPON. What are you doing in my bed sheet? Take it off at once. (LADY *proceeds to unwrap herself.*) Keep it on.

LADY. Your wish is my command. I am paid to please and I please when I've been paid.

PETIPON. What are you suggesting?

LADY. Whatever you have in mind.

MONGICOURT. I know you!

LADY. You know me?

MONGICOURT. I've seen you.

LADY. You've seen me?

SONG: LADY FROM MAXIM'S

I'm the Lady from Maxim's,
The face that smiles at you in dreams,
The finger beckoning to romance,
The arms that dare you: Take a chance!

I've well-bred ankles and a mocking eye
For each monsieur who passes by.
I'm a coquette and very bold,
But I'm not yours to have or hold.

Though my life is très, très bohème
And I could be a very fatal femme,
Yet I'm demure and slightly shy.
There's more in me than meets the eye!

And if I whisper "Ah, toujours l'amour"
You'll have to come much closer to be sure.
She is seldom what she seems.
You know her as the Lady from Maxim's.

PETIPON. Do we know each other? Have we ever been introduced?

LADY. We know each other, but we've never been introduced.

MONGICOURT. Fascinating, fascinating. I am Dr. Mongicourt. Ah, that is Dr. Petipon. "Fascinating" is wrong—misleading. You should be billed as Adorable—Incredible

—Unbelievable—Superb— (*He is breathing hard at this moment.*)

LADY. Calm yourself, Doctor.

MADAME PETIPON. (*Offstage.*) Etienne!

PETIPON. Gabrielle! Gabrielle! What shame have I introduced you to? Gabrielle! Gabrielle! I am a cur—I am a dog!

MONGICOURT. What are you ranting about?

PETIPON. I've introduced my wife to shame!

LADY. I assure you we've never met—

PETIPON. Gabrielle kissed her!

MONGICOURT. Where?

PETIPON. On the forehead.

MONGICOURT. Fate plays absurd tricks on us all. . . . That forehead wasted on your Gabrielle. That square inch of perfect flesh was meant for the lips of a connoisseur— me.

LADY. But you didn't bring me home, monsieur. He did.

MONGICOURT. I behaved like a cad. Can you forgive me?

LADY. (*Holds out her hand.*) Only with great effort.

MONGICOURT. Before you, all Mongicourt trembles.

MADAME ETIENNE. (*Offstage.*) Etienne!

PETIPON. Please tremble outside. My wife will return at any moment.

(MADAME PETIPON'S *voice is heard from offstage.*)

MADAME PETIPON. No lemons? My Lucien must have lemons.

PETIPON. She's too good for me.

ETIENNE. There were none this morning, madame.

MADAME PETIPON. Search all of Paris. My Lucien must have his lemons. An herbal tea is meaningless without lemons.

PETIPON. She *is* too good for me.

MONGICOURT. I'd wager that Madame Petipon is about to join us.

PETIPON. No.

MONGICOURT. Yes.

PETIPON. (*To* LADY.) Leave!

LADY. No!

PETIPON. At once! (*Points offstage.*)

MONGICOURT. Through that door?

PETIPON. Through that door! (*Looks, then reacts.*)
Hide.

LADY. Hide?

PETIPON. I order you to hide.

(MADAME PETIPON *enters* D. L., *carrying a tray with the
tea and accessories.* MONGICOURT *stands in front of*
LADY. MADAME PETIPON *does not see her, and
during the next few speeches,* MONGICOURT *maneu-
vers* LADY *into the sleeping alcove.*)

MADAME PETIPON. How is my soldier? Soon your
tummy will be bright as a penny!

MONGICOURT. Not a happy image!

PETIPON. Not very.

MONGICOURT. An unfortunate phrase.

MADAME PETIPON. Please remove that dress from the
table, my dear.

PETIPON. Dress?

MONGICOURT. (*Crosses.*) Dress?

PETIPON. What dress?

MADAME PETIPON. That dress!

PETIPON. It is a tablecloth.

MADAME PETIPON. It is a dress!

PETIPON. Cloth!

MADAME PETIPON. Dress!

PETIPON. Cloth!

MADAME PETIPON. Dress!

PETIPON. Whose dress?

MADAME PETIPON. (*Has placed the tray on the table
and snatches the dress from* PETIPON.) My dress!

MONGICOURT. Her dress?

MADAME PETIPON. When did it arrive?

MONGICOURT. It was here when I entered the room.

PETIPON. I remember nothing—my life is flashing before my eyes like a drowning man. I'm quite dizzy—as a matter of fact I intend to faint!

MADAME PETIPON. How really wicked!

PETIPON. I am not responsible for my physical condition.

MADAME PETIPON. I was referring to Madame Claude, my dressmaker. . . . The dress is a day late—neither color or style that I ordered—and arrives sans the discretion of a box.

PETIPON. Give it to me. (*Grabs it from* MADAME PETIPON.)

MONGICOURT. It won't suit you any better than it does Madame Petipon. (*Holds it from* PETIPON.)

PETIPON. I shall return it personally—and personally reprimand Madame Claude. (*Grabs it from* MONGICOURT.)

MADAME PETIPON. I appreciate your concern, but I will attend to the matter myself. (*Grabs the dress from* PETIPON *and exits.*)

(LADY *storms out of the alcove.*)

PETIPON. Where are you going?

LADY. To get my dress back.

PETIPON. Oh, no, you're not.

LADY. Oh, yes, I am.

PETIPON. Oh, no, you're not.

MONGICOURT. You wouldn't.

LADY. Oh, yes, I am. (*Dodges around* PETIPON.)

MONGICOURT. Oh, yes, she is.

PETIPON. Pity!

LADY. Stop it.

PETIPON. Madame, I assure you—

LADY. Don't appeal to my tender heart—you know how sentimental I am.

PETIPON. I know nothing! This is a dream—a dream—and I shall awaken to discover that that fascinating creature was but a Camembert too ripe to eat—

MONGICOURT. And I? What am I in this dream?

PETIPON. A liver pâté that has soured.

MONGICOURT. That is an ugly image—

LADY. You didn't tell me that you were married. The fee for a married man is double—

PETIPON. How much do I owe you?

LADY. I want everything you promised!

MONGICOURT. He promised you—

LADY. Marriage, monsieur. It would have been beautiful—our marriage. I would have been a perfect wife. Where else could he have found a woman of my tender years with the richness of my experience, my skill at pleasing a man? Oh—

MONGICOURT. What is the matter?

LADY. I feel so—so—

MONGICOURT. You feel so?

LADY. Japanese.

MONGICOURT. I don't know the remedy for that.

LADY. Marriage would cure everything.

PETIPON. She lies— I promised nothing—

LADY. I lie? You lie! You said you had no memory of what to me was a rapturous evening. Oh, I'll leave. I know when I've been insulted.

PETIPON. How much do I owe you?

LADY. I couldn't accept money from you now. If you have forgotten, as you say you have, you owe me nothing—

PETIPON. Good-bye.

LADY. Except compensation for the loss of my dress.

MONGICOURT. That's only fair.

LADY. Thank you, monsieur. You have a sensitivity that a woman appreciates.

PETIPON. How much for the dress?

LADY. It was an original model.

PETIPON. The sum? The sum!

LADY. The only one of its kind.

PETIPON. 40 francs? Will 40 francs cover it?

LADY. 40 francs?

PETIPON. (*Starts to count out the money.*) 20—30—yes—40 francs.

LADY. Dr. Mongicourt? Do you hear? Have you any idea how hard I had to work to earn that dress?

PETIPON. I don't think I want to know.

LADY. It cost me 1,000 francs and I'm not going till I get my dress back.

(*From offstage we hear* MADAME PETIPON'S *voice. As she enters, hands over eyes, deeply emotionally moved,* PETIPON *and* MONGICOURT *pick up* LADY *and rush her into the alcove, drop her on the bed and resume attentive, respectful positions so that* MADAME PETIPON *has not seen any of their physical action.*)

MADAME PETIPON. Lucien Petipon, I saw her. Unbelievable, celestial vision! I saw her.

PETIPON. I've a confession to make.

MADAME PETIPON. Yes, that's it—confession. When confronted one confesses—or does one confess then become confronted?

PETIPON. You won't believe this—

MADAME PETIPON. I do. I do. I'm so pleased, so pleased that you believe.

MONGICOURT. Good Lord.

MADAME PETIPON. How true! The good Lord is responsible—

PETIPON. For your seeing her?

MADAME PETIPON. I saw her in the kitchen—

MONGICOURT. In the kitchen?

MADAME PETIPON. Hovering over the onions and the garlic cloves—

PETIPON. Whom did you see?

MADAME PETIPON. St. Catherine—

MONGICOURT. ST. CATHERINE?

PETIPON. St. Catherine! She appears only to special people. Not to just anyone.

MONGICOURT. And you saw St. Catherine?

MADAME PETIPON. And heard her. I'm to receive a VISITATION. An angel is going to address me. St. Catherine told me to be prepared.

LADY. GABRIELLE? Gabrielle!

MADAME PETIPON. So soon?

LADY. Gabrielle!

(LADY *appears in the entrance of the alcove mysteriously draped in the bed sheets and with a mystical light behind her.*)

MADAME PETIPON. Ah, do you see?

PETIPON. Who?

MADAME PETIPON. The angel.

LADY. They can not see me—they can not hear me. Only you, Gabrielle, are pure of heart.

MADAME PETIPON. But only a moment ago Lucien was speaking of confession. Forgive him. His will is strong but his flesh is weak.

LADY. I know!

(MONGICOURT *bursts out laughing.*)

MADAME PETIPON. Kneel. Kneel . . .

(*The three are kneeling as* ETIENNE *enters, carrying a lemon and a small silver tray.*)

ETIENNE. Well, I'll be damned.

MONGICOURT. More than likely.

MADAME PETIPON. Kneel, Etienne, kneel for the sake of your immortal soul.

ETIENNE. Who is that?

MADAME PETIPON. You see it?

ETIENNE. I see it. What is it?

MADAME PETIPON. You are one of the chosen few. It is an archangel from on high.

LADY. GABRIELLE! ATTEND ME! LISTEN TO YOUR DESTINY!

MADAME PETIPON. Command me. I obey.

ETIENNE. Command her. She'll obey.

LADY. When I have completed my message . . . you will act at once. Without delay you will follow my instructions to the letter.

MADAME PETIPON. To the letter.

ETIENNE. To the letter.

LADY. Leave the house. Hasten to the Place de la Concorde. Circle it five times—

MADAME PETIPON. I circle it five times.

ETIENNE. You circle it five times—

LADY. When you have completed this ritual, praying all the while, a prayer of your own choice, wait at the Obelisque until a man speaks to you. . . .

MADAME PETIPON. What man?

LADY. The first man who speaks to you will be the man who will shape your destiny. Receive his word with a pure heart—that word will be made flesh and that flesh will be a son that will be born unto you—

MADAME PETIPON. Unto me?

LADY. Unto you!

ETIENNE. Unto she—her—Madame—

PETIPON. Shut up—

MADAME PETIPON. How dare you speak to an archangel like that!

PETIPON. I was talking to Etienne—

LADY. The son that shall be born unto you—will restore the monarchy and rule France. Unto you will be born a king. Go, Gabrielle, for France.

MADAME PETIPON. (*Rises. Starts to leave. Stops. Turns.*) The Place de la Concorde?

ETIENNE. That's what she said.

LADY. Take thy servant with thee.

MADAME PETIPON. With me? To the Place de la Concorde?

LADY. No, just from this room! He is never to cross that doorsill again. It is written.

MADAME PETIPON. I obey for France. (*She exits* D. R.)

ETIENNE. We obey for France. (*He exits* D. R.)

MONGICOURT. Brilliant! Brilliant acting! And to think she wastes her talents . . .

LADY. Careful, monsieur.

MONGICOURT. As a dancer.

LADY. Now go . . . go.

PETIPON. Ordered out of my own home?

LADY. Go and get me some clothes. Unless of course you want me to remain until your wife returns?

PETIPON. I obey.—Mongicourt!

MONGICOURT. We obey.

(*They exit.*)

GENERAL. (*Offstage.*) Is this the house of Dr. Petipon?

LADY. Who can that be?

GENERAL. (*From offstage.*) Tell Dr. Petipon that it is his uncle General Petipon who wishes to be received.

ETIENNE. This way, mon general.

(*The* GENERAL *strides into the room.*)

GENERAL. No one here. Why do you loiter there in the entrance?

ETIENNE. I have been commanded by a higher power not to cross this threshold.

GENERAL. So, my nephew is harsh with the servants. Where is he?

ETIENNE. His habits are not very regular of late. I suggest that you look under the furniture. (*Exits.*)

(*During the next speech, the* GENERAL *wanders about the room looking for his nephew. When he enters the sleeping alcove he sees* LADY's *rear end raised in the air beneath the sheets and he takes a mighty slap at it.*)

GENERAL. Lucien? Lucien? Where are you, boy? Now, Lucien, don't play games with me or I'll—ah, there you are! (*Delivers a mighty slap.* LADY *leaps up indignantly.*)

LADY. How dare you! (*Shrieks.*) How dare you attack me—and we haven't even been introduced!

GENERAL. Forgive me. I had no idea— I thought it was Lucien—my nephew—

LADY. Strange games for men to play.

GENERAL. I am not a man—I am an uncle. You must be my niece Gabrielle. Good afternoon, my dear.

LADY. How do you do?

GENERAL. Fine actually. My bursitis has cleared up. Nine years in darkest Africa had almost done me in. And now I've returned to find Lucien married to a charming creature.

LADY. And who are you, monsieur?

GENERAL. You must have heard of me. I am your uncle General Baron Petipon de la Grele.

LADY. And I am—

GENERAL. No need for introductions. I feel that we know each other quite well already and will be friends— forever. Are you ill?

LADY. I'm quite well, thank you.

GENERAL. Then I've awakened you.

LADY. Oh, this? You mean my casual attire? You've been away a long time, uncle. It's very much the fashion of the moment.

GENERAL. I must tell Clementine. She's such a country girl. But so teachable.

LADY. Clementine?

GENERAL. My niece, your cousin, Clementine Bourre? The dear child I adopted when her poor parents died. We need you, Clementine and I.

LADY. What do you have in mind?

GENERAL. She needs a mother. I'm marrying her off and she needs a mother at her side. She's to be married in a week to Lieutenant Corignon.

LADY. She—Clementine—married to Corignon of the 12th Dragoons?

GENERAL. You know him then?

LADY. Know him? Never heard of him! Or indeed of the 12th Dragoons.

GENERAL. Then you shall meet him. Tomorrow when we sign the marriage contracts at my chateau in Touraine. You'll meet him then. You're going to be my hostess and help me to get the child married off in style.

LADY. It might be amusing.

GENERAL. Then you'll help me?

LADY. I shall help you.

GENERAL. So generous, so warm, so responsive to my needs. What a family! What a dear sweet girl! (*Kisses* LADY.)

LADY. Ah, mon Général, the heat and mists of Africa have not dampened your ardor.

GENERAL. Nine years of Africa might destroy enlisted men. *Generals* are inspired to excel themselves.

(*The* GENERAL *sings a marching song to* LADY. *At conclusion of song* PETIPON *enters. He walks fussily up to the* GENERAL *and speaks to him casually as if resuming an interrupted conversation.*)

GENERAL'S SONG

(Allons, enfants le la patrie.
Le jour de gloire est arrivé [Instrumental].)

My victories on foreign strands
Were sorties strong and bold
But the victories I won in bed
Are the ones to which I hold.

And the medals on my chest
And the trophies on my walls
Tell the glorious story of my life,
A tale that never palls.

(Allons, enfants, etc.)

My dossier as a young cadet
Was rich and variegated.
My campaigns on strange terrains
With panache were consummated.

And the medals, etc.

My conquests made in foreign lands
Were tender and exotic,
My simplest wishes were commands,
My glances were hypnotic.

And the medals, etc.

I rose in rank right to the top,
Each skirmish took me higher.
Citations read: Intrepid man
And gallant under fire.

And the medals, etc.

Now for the first time in my life
I negotiate for peace.
The lady is my nephew's wife;
Ergo, she is my niece.

And the medals, etc.

PETIPON. Everything is at sixes and sevens. That damned fool Etienne can't find my kaftan or fez. I can't find a suitable dress among my wife's things—and with all the confusion in this house today it's no wonder that my head's reeling. How are you?

GENERAL. Fine, and you?

PETIPON. As I said—at sixes and sevens.

GENERAL. You're not surprised to see me?

PETIPON. Surprised?

GENERAL. It's been almost ten years.

PETIPON. Ten years?

GENERAL. Ten years!

PETIPON. I can't believe it!

GENERAL. As they say—"Time—"

PETIPON. Flies— Oh, my God! What are you doing here? You belong in Africa!

GENERAL. Kiss me, you fool. What are you waiting for?

(*The men exchange kisses on both cheeks. In conclusion the* GENERAL *removes a medal from the row on his chest and pins it to* PETIPON'S.)

PETIPON. And how long are you going to be with us?

GENERAL. An hour. 58 and ½ minutes to be exact.

PETIPON. Excellent.

GENERAL. I'll leave now if that's what you wish.

PETIPON. I couldn't bear it. Please stay.

GENERAL. I can't. But you and your dear wife can come with me to Touraine.

PETIPON. To Touraine?

GENERAL. To Touraine.

PETIPON. I'll ask her.

GENERAL. But she's agreed.

LADY. I've agreed.

PETIPON. You've agreed.

GENERAL. She's agreed.

PETIPON. That woman is not my wife!

GENERAL. Not your wife? How long have you been living together?

PETIPON. Eight years.

GENERAL. And not married. It's a good thing for you

that I'm a hardened old soldier. You'll have to remedy the situation, you know.

PETIPON. I am married. But not to her.

GENERAL. What?

LADY. A bigamist. The man is shameless.

(*The* GENERAL *tears a page out of a sleeve cuff.*)

PETIPON. What are you doing?

GENERAL. I am cutting you out of my will. Fetch the servant.

PETIPON. (*Calls.*) Etienne. Etienne! Why does he want Etienne?

GENERAL. To establish whether this lady is your wife or not.

PETIPON. She's my wife.

LADY. A moment ago you said . . .

PETIPON. Aren't I famous for my practical jokes? Surely you remember that I'm considered quite a card? Don't I have the greatest sense of humor you've ever encountered?

(*Knock is heard offstage.*)

GENERAL. Come in.

PETIPON. Go away.

GENERAL. Come in.

PETIPON. We don't want any.

(ETIENNE *enters* D. R. *carrying a dress box.*)

ETIENNE. A package, monsieur, for madame from the dressmaker.

GENERAL. Ah— Ah— Ah— Ah— Ah— It is all very clear—

PETIPON. Excellent diagnosis—it doesn't sound like a congestion to me.

GENERAL. The box!

PETIPON. The box?

GENERAL. Madame's box!

PETIPON. Madame's box?

GENERAL. It clearly establishes that madame is your wife—and that you are married and were jesting and I think it's a hell of a way to treat an old soldier, let alone a man who has returned from darkest Africa after nine long years of tropical fevers and pounding drums.

LADY. Lucien, you're so inconsiderate. I'll comfort you, dear uncle.

PETIPON. But your dress— (*Hands her the dress box.*)

LADY. Thank you. (*Opens the box. Takes a dress from it.*)

GENERAL. (*To* PETIPON.) She's too young for you, you know.

PETIPON. I'm afraid you are right.

GENERAL. Much too energetic and vibrant for a man of your advanced years.

PETIPON. See here—who is the nephew and who is the uncle?

GENERAL. I'm beginning to wonder. No matter— I'm certain of one thing—that girl is going to electrify Touraine.

(MONGICOURT *enters* D. R. *with packages.*)

MONGICOURT. (*Sees the* GENERAL.) Wrong house. (*Starts to leave* D. R.)

PETIPON. Nonsense, dear Mongicourt. Allow me to introduce you to my uncle, General Petipon of Grele.

MONGICOURT. Of course. How do you do?

GENERAL. I'm in a hurry actually, must leave for Touraine to marry off a niece. Incidentally, Lucien, as I told Madame Petipon, dear Clementine is marrying Lieutenant Corignon.

MONGICOURT. Oh, she's returned?

GENERAL. Clementine?

MONGICOURT. Madame Petipon.

GENERAL. She's dressing in there.

MONGICOURT. In there?

GENERAL. Where else? (MADAME PETIPON'S *voice is heard from offstage.*) Etienne! Etienne! Help me. Help me. I faint with fatigue.

MADAME PETIPON. (*Enters* D. R.) Oh, I didn't know that it would be so exhausting.

PETIPON. What was exhausting?

MADAME PETIPON. I've been consecrated! If that's not exhausting what is?

PETIPON. I want you to meet my uncle—General Petipon of Grele.

MADAME PETIPON. I've heard so much about you— I must embrace you. (*Kisses the* GENERAL *on both cheeks and he with a gesture that is competely automatic pins a medal on her chest. To* PETIPON.) I'm pregnant!

GENERAL. Surely madame is not holding me responsible?

MADAME PETIPON. I did as I was told. I stood in the Place de la Concorde and suddenly—there he was—

PETIPON. Who?

MADAME PETIPON. A policeman.

PETIPON. What did he say?

MADAME PETIPON. "Watch it, girlie. No soliciting on the Champs Elysees!" Rather cryptic but I understood the message. I shall be Queen Mother. Oh the wonder of it! I must go to my room and meditate. If you need anything just ask my husband. You'll excuse me, General? (*Exits* D. L.)

GENERAL. Her husband?

PETIPON. Her husband?

MONGICOURT. Her husband?

GENERAL. (*To* MONGICOURT.) Oh, I understand. Madame is your wife!

PETIPON. I had forgotten. Of course Madame Mongicourt is Dr. Mongicourt's wife.

MONGICOURT. My wife?

PETIPON. Ah, you see? He admits it. Of course. She is your wife.

(LADY *enters from the sleeping alcove dressed in* GA-
BRIELLE'S *new dress.*)

GENERAL. And here is your wife. I have to run, my
dear. Remember now, we meet promptly at the station at
4:05.

LADY. Promptly! Have no fear.

GENERAL. Although we meet again in less than one hour
I must kiss you. (LADY *and the* GENERAL *embrace. He
pins an entire row of medals to her dress. To* MONGI-
COURT:) You've got to admit it, Lucien has the same
taste as his old uncle when it comes to women. (*Chuckles
as he exits* D. R.)

PETIPON. I want to thank you, madame.

LADY. It's about time.

PETIPON. For the mess you've created.

LADY. Don't give me all of the credit. I had some help
from you.

PETIPON. How could you?

LADY. It was easy. Shall we call Gabrielle in and explain things to her?

PETIPON. Such as—?

LADY. What is meant by the cryptic phrase "soliciting."

MONGICOURT. What are you two upset about? At least
you have each other. I've been left with dear Gabrielle.

PETIPON. How dare you speak of my wife in that tone
of voice?

MONGICOURT. Your wife?

PETIPON. My wife!

MONGICOURT. My wife! Damn it. You married her off
to me.

PETIPON. (*To* LADY.) Where are you going?

LADY. Home to pack. We have a rendezvous, remember? 4:05 P.M. at the station—the train for Touraine and
all points south to uncle's chateau. (*Exits.*)

SONG: WHO WAS THAT LADY? or, TROUBLE AND STRIFE

PETIPON.
  Oh!
MONGICOURT.
  Oh!
PETIPON.
  Woe!
MONGICOURT.
  Woe!

MONGICOURT AND PETIPON.
  Who was that lady?
MONGICOURT.
  That was my wife.
PETIPON.
  That was my wife.
MONGICOURT AND PETIPON.
  He's right, it was his wife.

PETIPON.
  But yesterday, I had no worries—
  I had no sons, I had no daughters.
MONGICOURT.
  His thirst was quenched with mineral waters!

MONGICOURT.
  But yesterday, I had no worries—
  I practiced daily at my clinic.
PETIPON.
  A thoroughgoing, hardened cynic!

MONGICOURT AND PETIPON.
  Today we're both at sixes and sevens.
  Retribution rained from the heavens
  And now we're stuck for good or ill—
PETIPON.
  At least till the General makes his will!

MONGICOURT AND PETIPON.
   Trouble and strife,
   Trouble and strife.
   That was no lady,
   That was *our* wife!

(ETIENNE *enters, wheeling in the ecstatic armchair, covered.*)

ETIENNE. Where does this object go?

PETIPON. Leave it there. With all this confusion I'd forgotten all about it.

MONGICOURT. What is it—a corpse?

PETIPON. My ecstatic armchair—

MONGICOURT. Your what?

PETIPON. My ecstatic armchair. The latest invention from Vienna.

MONGICOURT. What does it do? Vibrate?

PETIPON. Better than that—push the right switches and the patient is in painless Paradise. Something like a dentist's laughing gas, only better. (PETIPON *has removed a box from beneath the cloth, opened it, set the machine in operation by hooking it up electrically and has also taken a pair of green insulated gloves from the package.*)

MONGICOURT. What are those gloves for?

PETIPON. To protect the operator of the machine.

MONGICOURT. Looks harmless enough. (*Sits in it.*) Very comfortable, very comfortable. Surely it's only a barber's chair.

PETIPON. This switch on the left activates the machine—and the switch on the right turns it off—

MONGICOURT. Surely it's nothing but a— (*Makes a sweeping gesture and activates the machine. His usually sullen face is suddenly wreathed in smiles.*)

(PETIPON *has crossed* D. L. *and calls offstage for his wife.*)

PETIPON. Gabrielle! Gabrielle?

MADAME PETIPON. (*Appears immediately.*) You called?

PETIPON. My ecstatic machine is here.

MADAME PETIPON. Where?

PETIPON. There. (*Turns and sees* MONGICOURT.)

MADAME PETIPON. What's the matter with Dr. Mongicourt?

PETIPON. Dr. Mongicourt. I'll be damned. He's activated the machine. Aha! Now you'll take it seriously, Mongicourt. You old quack.

MADAME PETIPON. You'll offend Dr. Mongicourt. Please excuse my husband, Doctor.

PETIPON. He hears nothing. He sees nothing. You could saw an arm off and he'd feel nothing. . . . I could operate—

MADAME PETIPON. Operate?

PETIPON. Oh, thank you for reminding me—please pack a small suitcase for me. I have to leave in 15 minutes—

MADAME PETIPON. In 15 minutes?

PETIPON. A major operation. I've been called out of town—and when duty calls one has to go.

MADAME PETIPON. So I found out today—

PETIPON. You found out?

MADAME PETIPON. When I was summoned to be consecrated as a holy receptacle. I'll pack for you, my dear.

PETIPON. You do that. (*She exits* U. L. PETIPON *crosses and looks down at* MONGICOURT.) Ye of little faith.

ETIENNE. (*From offstage.*) One moment, sir. I must announce you. And even then I'm not sure Dr. Petipon will receive you.

CORIGNON. (*Enters* D. R.) Have they been here? Doctor, have they been here?

PETIPON. Who?

CORIGNON. My seconds.

PETIPON. Your what?

CORIGNON. SECONDS!

PETIPON. Seconds?

CORIGNON. Don't you understand?

PETIPON. Understand?

CORIGNON. I just found out who you are.

PETIPON. Who am I?

ETIENNE. You are Dr. Petipon and he is Lt. Alexandre Corignon.

CORIGNON. You are the dear cousin of my dear Clementine. I can't kill you.

PETIPON. Can't kill me?

CORIGNON. I can't kill you.

PETIPON. Why can't you kill me?

CORIGNON. We're to be married.

PETIPON. Married?

CORIGNON. Clementine and I.

PETIPON. And?

CORIGNON. Last night!

PETIPON. What about last night?

CORIGNON. Last night at Maxim's, when I discovered you with my mistress, I challenged you and you said, "Name your seconds!" Have they been here?

PETIPON. No. But be patient—they'll show up. Everyone else in Paris has.

CORIGNON. I can't kill you now.

PETIPON. But a challenge is a challenge and we've our honor to consider.

CORIGNON. That will have to wait—until after tomorrow. General Petipon said that we're to meet at the train at 4:05 and I don't want to make a bad impression —not this early in the game.

PETIPON. The train. I've forgotten. You must go. No, I must go— Gabrielle! (*Calls again.*) Gabrielle?

CORIGNON. Until we meet at the station.

PETIPON. Until we meet at the station.

(CORIGNON *rushes from the room as* GABRIELLE *enters with a small suitcase* U. L.)

MADAME PETIPON. Who was that?

PETIPON. The patient's mistress!

MADAME PETIPON. Mistress?

PETIPON. Son, son, urging me to hurry. The patient has reached a crisis and only I can save him. I'm late—suitcase all packed?

MADAME PETIPON. All packed. Oh, this letter came for you—

PETIPON. I don't have time to read it now.

MADAME PETIPON. It's addressed to both of us—

PETIPON. Read it. When I return you can tell me what it says. Where's my medical bag?

MADAME PETIPON. In the surgery where you left it. (*Opens the letter and reads it aloud.*) So— The General asks us to visit him in Touraine and to assist in the engagement and marriage of dear Clementine. Why didn't he mention it when he was here? If he wants me to be his hostess—the polite thing would have been to ask me personally. Well—since Lucien is called away on this case I shall have to serve alone—but serve I shall. Family duty is family duty. (PETIPON *returns dressed to go out.*) Lucien, you'll never guess whom the letter is from!

PETIPON. Later, not now, later.

MADAME PETIPON. But you should know. Since he didn't mention a word of it—

PETIPON. Later, I said. Later.

(*The* GENERAL'S *voice is heard offstage.*)

GENERAL. Tell my nephew I've decided to drive him to the station in my cab— There's room for all.

MADAME PETIPON. Isn't that—?

PETIPON. No, it isn't. Rest yourself, my dear. Lie down in the Turkish corner. Take a nap. Meditate.

MADAME PETIPON. I'm not tired. I tell you, not tired. Lucien, what's gotten into you! Take your hand off of my arm— (*Pulls away and falls backward onto* MONGICOURT'S *lap. Her face freezes in an astounded expression, mouth open.*)

GENERAL. Lucien— I'm waiting. Lucien—we've a train to catch.

PETIPON. (*Takes cloth that had covered chair and covers* MONGICOURT *and* GABRIELLE.) Uncle? Is that you, Uncle?

GENERAL. (*Enters* D. R.) Let's go.

PETIPON. I'm ready.

GENERAL. (*Points to chair.*) What's that?

PETIPON. An anatomical figure.

GENERAL. Let me see it.

PETIPON. No. Wet paint. Must allow it to dry undisturbed. (*Pushes him toward the door.*) Wait for me in the cab. I'll be right out.

(ETIENNE *enters with the street cleaner* D. R.)

ETIENNE. This gentleman claims that he is expected.

CLEANER. You can say that again.

ETIENNE. He claims that he is expected.

PETIPON. Who are you?

CLEANER. The cleaner from the Rue Royale.

PETIPON. What do you want?

CLEANER. You invited me to dinner.

PETIPON. I?

CLEANER. Last night!

PETIPON. I probably did.

CLEANER. Here's the card you gave me. When I picked you up out of the gutter. You had fallen, you see—

PETIPON. Oh, what a great fall that was, my friend. Get out, Etienne. Out, out, now. And tell the General I'll only be a moment. (ETIENNE *exits* D. R. *To* CLEANER:) I'm going to instruct the servants to feast you.

CLEANER. Thank you, monsieur.

PETIPON. But first a little favor.

CLEANER. Yes, monsieur?

PETIPON. When I leave, the exact moment I'm out of that door, I want you to press this switch. (*Shows* CLEANER *button on right side of chair.*) Eh, eh? The exact moment that I leave. Understand?

CLEANER. Yes, monsieur. Command me. I obey.

PETIPON. Farewell. (*Exits* D. R.) Gabrielle.

CLEANER. My name is Pierre, monsieur. (*Presses the switch. A shriek is heard. He pulls the sheet from the chair.* MADAME PETIPON *is struggling to get out of the chair.*)

MADAME PETIPON. (*To* MONGICOURT.) How dare you, monsieur. Wait until my husband hears of this. (*To* CLEANER.) And who are you?

CLEANER. Your dinner guest.

MADAME PETIPON. My what?

CLEANER. Dinner guest. I'm hungry.

MADAME PETIPON. Etienne. Etienne.

MONGICOURT. I remember nothing.

ETIENNE. Yes, madame—what is it?

MADAME PETIPON. I've been attacked by these two beasts.

CLEANER. I want my supper.

MONGICOURT. I remember nothing.

CLEANER. (*Struggles to explain to* GABRIELLE *who retreats from him.*) I want my supper. I've been promised supper.

MONGICOURT. I want my attorney. I want my attorney.

CLEANER. I want my supper. . . .

(ETIENNE *tries to carry the struggling* CLEANER *from the room.*)

MONGICOURT. I plead insanity—total loss of memory—

CLEANER. I want my supper—

ETIENNE. This house has gone mad!

MADAME PETIPON. (*Kneels* L.) Oh, dear St. Catherine, are you testing me with these trials and tribulations?

CLEANER. I want my suppp-er—

CURTAIN

ACT TWO

Scene 1

A garden on the General's *estate at Grele. Stage* c. *a round garden bench. The* Village Priest *of Grele enters with his assistant,* Brother Julian. *It is a bright spring afternoon and the morning dew seems to have lingered lovingly in this charming place.*

Priest. Ah, Brother Julian, it is indeed fortunate that that lovely child Clementine has at last been reached by a ray of God's beneficence—

Julian. Considering the tragedy of her poor parents' death—

Priest. Spare me, spare me—no details. I shudder when I think of the horror of their passing. Yet—Clementine—dear child, has regained her warm good spirits and the fates are smiling—yes, smiling at last upon her—

Julian. You refer of course to Lt. Corignon—

Priest. Corignon—a perfect companion for our Clementine—

Julian. And Simone?

Priest. The dear child will miss her adopted sister. Our Simone goes to a convent—of her own volition. I do believe she has a vocation—

Julian. Where are the dear children?

Priest. Clementine and Corignon?

Julian. How romantic you are, Father. No, no, I refer to our young ladies—

Priest. Choose a garden path and at its end you'll find them studying in a bower or a nook their Latin or Greek, or even what has become quite daring these days—daring in the sense that young ladies are becoming so bold and venturesome — MATHEMATICS — Higher MATHEMATICS—

39

JULIAN. I shall seek them out—

PRIEST. Do that whilst I remain behind for a moment to commune with God and nature—

JULIAN. Very well, Father.

PRIEST. Good morning—trees—birds—bees—flowers. What a lovely moment God's inspiration has created for us. What is that little bird? No—no—no— I am not worthy—do not confess unto me. I am no St. Francis. I am unworthy of your confidence; find a humble man and speak unto him. I am too much with the world, too much—

(BROTHER JULIAN *returns by another path.*)

JULIAN. I found them. I found them—and you were wrong, Father—they were pursuing a subject much more alarming than mathematics—

(CLEMENTINE *and* SIMONE *enter. They carry a picnic basket and books.*)

CLEMENTINE. Geometry— We were keeping our world from spinning off of its axis by studying geometry. Will you hear our confessions today, Father?

PRIEST. Pure of heart—what confessions?

CLEMENTINE. Mine and Lt. Corignon's—

SIMONE. Clementine!

JULIAN. Do you not blush, dear child?

PRIEST. I quite understand—Simone's shock and Clementine's blush. The linking of the names Clementine and Lt. Corignon is daring—bold—and here I chide you, child—inappropriate—

JULIAN. Inappropriate, Father?

CLEMENTINE. Brother Julian, I understand. It was wrong of me to use the lieutenant's name so intimately. You see, we are not yet formally engaged.

PRIEST. Perhaps I am too harsh. It is only a matter of hours and then you may use his name as freely as if it were your own because surely soon it will indeed be your own—

(SIMONE *whispers to* CLEMENTINE.)

CLEMENTINE. You ask Father.
SIMONE. You—
CLEMENTINE. But it was your question?
PRIEST. Ask me what, child?
CLEMENTINE. I can't.
SIMONE. Ask him.
JULIAN. Be careful—you know how unworldly our dear father is.
PRIEST. Now you frighten me.
CLEMENTINE. Whisper your question to Father, dear Simone.

(SIMONE *does so.*)

PRIEST. Lt. Corignon's Christian name is Alexandre.
SIMONE. Alexandre.
CLEMENTINE. Alexandre— How sensual. Alexandre— Alexandre. Simone, I shall no longer be your dear friend and companion, Clementine Bourre. Shortly I will become Madame Alexandre Corignon. I am frightened.
SIMONE. Oh, look what you have done—
JULIAN. You've crushed the dainty flower that you had picked so lovingly as we walked back here down that twining path—

(*The* GENERAL, *the* LADY *and* PETIPON *enter.*)

GENERAL. Our guests are arriving, Clementine. We are fortunate that Dr. and Madame Petipon have been here to greet them.
PRIEST. The dear children were quite lost amid their studies and had forgotten the hour.
GENERAL. Madame Petipon has brought a breath of Paris air to our village—

PETIPON. I'm grateful that Paris is behind us.

GENERAL. You see, nephew? I was right—you needed a change—

LADY. He doesn't agree with you.

PETIPON. I disagree with my uncle? I? Never—

GENERAL. Then you'll allow me to escort madame to our luncheon?

PETIPON. By all means—by all means. And I shall take your young charges under my wing—

LADY. They couldn't be in safer company.

PETIPON. What do you mean by that?

PRIEST. The light-hearted banter of a happily married couple never ceases to charm me—

CLEMENTINE. Dear cousin Lucien, we mustn't neglect our guests. Come, Simone.

SIMONE. Father, Brother Julian— (PETIPON *and the* TWO GIRLS *followed by the* PRIEST *and* BROTHER JULIAN *exit* D. L.)

GENERAL. At last we are alone.

LADY. Surely you jest. Yes, you jest—I do hope you jest—if not I should become quite alarmed.

GENERAL. I wish to express my gratitude. I have a gift for you—a gift that was always intended for Lucien's wife. Allow me, my dear—

LADY. Pearls!

GENERAL. You are the fifth generation of Petipon wives to wear the famous Petipon pearls. How warm and alive they seem against your skin—

LADY. I am overcome with emotion— (*She swoons into his arms.*)

GENERAL. Had I but known—

(*A voice is heard from offstage.*)

DUKE. Where is she? Where is she? I must see this fantastic creature with my own eyes. (*Enters.*) Pardon me, General—

GENERAL. Madame Petipon, may I introduce Le Duc de Valmonte?

LADY. How do you do?

DUKE. How do you do. Yes, yes—she is all I was led to believe she was—

LADY. And that is?

DUKE. Oh, she has put Madame Chantelle's nose out of joint—she positively loathes her.

GENERAL. Delicicus—

DUKE. So amusing—

LADY. Really, gentlemen.

GENERAL. Excuse me, my dear. You see, until now Madame Chantelle was our arbiter of Parisian fashion and manners—

DUKE. And you, Madame Petipon, have put her into eclipse. And what galls her even more is that several gentlemen swear they've met you in Paris, but they can't recall exactly where. General?

GENERAL. Yes—

DUKE. May I have a word privately with madame— I am in the need of advice that only a woman of the world can impart—

GENERAL. See here—

LADY. I shall be quite comfortable—talking with the Duke if you wish to look to your guests, Uncle—

GENERAL. Oh? Oh—of course—of course—you'll excuse me— (*Exits.*)

(*A voice is heard calling* CLEMENTINE *from offstage.*)

LADY. We shan't be able to talk now.

DUKE. Where shall I find you?

LADY. I shall remain here—

DUKE. I mean in Paris—

LADY. Why, at Maxim's—

DUKE. Maxim's—

LADY. Dr. Petipon dislikes dining at home—

(DUKE *exits as* CORIGNON *enters.*)

CORIGNON. Clementine—

LADY. I am not Clementine—

CORIGNON. Why did you follow me here—how did you find me?

LADY. Exactly to whom do you think you are speaking?

CORIGNON. Stop playing games—

(BROTHER JULIAN *enters hurriedly.*)

JULIAN. Excuse me, Madame Petipon. I've come to fetch Father's missal—he's misplaced it, sainted man.

LADY. Alas, it is not here.

JULIAN. Perhaps he dropped it along one of the garden paths. (*Exits.*)

CORIGNON. Madame Petipon?

LADY. Ah, the fates, how strange are the games they play on us! Chou-chou, I am to be your aunt. You and your Clementine must come to me with all your many, many little problems, and like your wise old aunty I shall do my best to patch up your quarrels and answer those questions that come so naturally to all newlyweds—

CORIGNON. Won't you listen to me?

LADY. I'd listen but never believe a word you had to say—

CORIGNON. It's convenient—

LADY. The way you lie? The tales you invent?

CORIGNON. I don't love her—in fact I've never met her. It was arranged by my superior officer, the General.

LADY. And like all good soldiers you obey without question. Go away, Chou-chou—you bore me—

CORIGNON. Don't you understand? It will be a marriage of convenience. It will give me enough money to pay my gambling debts and enough money to take care of—

LADY. I don't really need you, my dear. I've a few irons of my own in the fire. Chou-chou, you are not as charming today as you were yesterday.

JULIAN. Eureka, eureka! Oh, happy, happy day! We've found it, we've found it!

(BROTHER JULIAN *enters with* SIMONE.)

LADY. Lt. Corignon, I want you to meet—

CORIGNON. Clementine. How could I not recognize her? Dear Clementine—

SIMONE. I am Simone, sir—

CORIGNON. Of course.

JULIAN. Mademoiselle Simone is dear Mademoiselle Clementine's companion—

LADY. And here is dear, dear Clementine— (CLEMENTINE *enters*.)

SIMONE. This is the lieutenant—

CLEMENTINE. I know—

CORIGNON. You knew? You recognized me?

CLEMENTINE. By your insignia, sir.

JULIAN. Come, Mademoiselle Simone. We'll tell the General that the lieutenant has arrived. (*They exit.*)

LADY. And I shall explore the estate. Perhaps there is still larger game as yet uncaught. (*Exits.*)

CORIGNON. I think we've been left alone—

CLEMENTINE. On purpose—

CORIGNON. To learn to know each other. Are you afraid of me, Clementine?

CLEMENTINE. Perhaps I should be, but I'm not.

CORIGNON. I'm afraid of you.

CLEMENTINE. Of me?

CORIGNON. Of your lovely eyes—and beautiful hair— They are traps set to snare me—

CLEMENTINE. In the books Simone and I read—lovers— Oh, excuse me—

CORIGNON. Blush, blush—devastate me.

CLEMENTINE. Men and women fall in love so easily— so simply—

CORIGNON. At first sight—

CLEMENTINE. At first sight.

CORIGNON. It's not possible—

CLEMENTINE. Most improbable— (*MUSIC—love song duet* [*"Tell Me the Answers"*].)

CORIGNON. And yet?

CLEMENTINE. And yet?

SONG: "TELL ME THE ANSWERS"
(*Love song duet.*)

CORIGNON.

How can I live without your smile?

CLEMENTINE.

Is there a reason birds won't sing?

CORIGNON.

What can I do that's worth the while?

CLEMENTINE.

Is there a land where love is king?

BOTH.

Tell me the answers,
Let them unfold.
Tell me that love
Will never grow old.

CLEMENTINE.

Does your heart beat for me alone?

CORIGNON.

Where is the life that late I led?

CLEMENTINE.

Will you be there to call my own?

CORIGNON.

Where has my freedom fled?

ALL.

Tell me the answers,
Let them unfold.
Tell me that love
Will never grow old.

CORIGNON.

How can I wait for joy to begin?

CLEMENTINE.

When is the moment two are one?

CORIGNON.

Will I long then for what has been?

CLEMENTINE.
Are all our troubles done?

BOTH.
Tell me the answers,
Let them unfold.
Tell me that love
Will never grow old.

(MONGICOURT'S *voice is heard offstage calling "Petipon, Petipon." The young lovers exit as* MONGICOURT *enters.*)

MONGICOURT. Petipon, Petipon. Where are you, man?
PETIPON. (*Enters.*) Mongicourt, dear old chap. So nice to see you.
MONGICOURT. She's here.
PETIPON. Who is here?
MONGICOURT. Madame Petipon.
PETIPON. And how charming she is. The delight of all eyes.
MONGICOURT. Madame Petipon?
PETIPON. Madame Petipon.
MONGICOURT. Gabrielle?
PETIPON. Safe in Paris!
MADAME PETIPON. (*From offstage.*) Uncle. Uncle. Uncle. Where are you?
PETIPON. No.
MONGICOURT. Yes.
PETIPON. Not possible.
MONGICOURT. I followed her all the way from Paris—to warn you.
PETIPON. Kill me.
MONGICOURT. You can't avoid the inevitable. Gabrielle is here and you must deal with her.
PETIPON. I'd rather not.
MONGICOURT. You better had.
MADAME PETIPON. (*Enters.*) WHAT ARE YOU DOING HERE?

PETIPON. Just the question I was about to ask.

MADAME PETIPON. The letter. I tried to tell you about the letter.

PETIPON. I just happened to drop by on my way to the consultation I told you of.

MADAME PETIPON. (*As the* GENERAL *enters.*) You told me nothing.

GENERAL. Lucien, you left Madame Petipon at the table.

MADAME PETIPON. Lucien, I am quite confused.

GENERAL. (*Escorting the* LADY.) Dr. Mongicourt, what a delightful surprise!

MONGICOURT. Allow me to introduce—

MADAME PETIPON. What is the General doing with a tart from Montmartre?

GENERAL. What was that?

PETIPON. Nothing, nothing.

GENERAL. Dr. Mongicourt—what did your wife just say?

MONGICOURT. My wife?

PETIPON. Your wife.

MONGICOURT. To be sure. My wife.

GENERAL. She said?

MONGICOURT. Who is that tart from Montmartre—

PETIPON. Mongicourt!

MONGICOURT. Oh, my God!

GENERAL. Step aside, nephew! If you are not man enough to defend your wife's honor, I am— I challenge you to a duel. You may name your weapons and your seconds—

MONGICOURT. A duel?

PETIPON. A duel.

GENERAL. To defend your wife's honor.

PETIPON. My wife?

LADY. Your wife.

MADAME PETIPON. His wife?

GENERAL. His wife.

MADAME PETIPON. I came to help—just as you requested, and I am greeted with insults and abuse.

GENERAL. The woman is mad. Quite mad.

MADAME PETIPON. How dare you, you beast!

MONGICOURT. I agree—she's quite mad.

GENERAL. Nevertheless—we duel. I shall ask Lt. Corignon to second me. Come, we've arrangements to make— (*Exits.*)

MONGICOURT. Petipon, you shall be the death of me.

PETIPON. You have placed Dr. Mongicourt's life in jeopardy. Follow them, madame, and try to make amends.

MADAME PETIPON. (*As she follows him.*) I don't understand— I don't understand—

PETIPON. I'm dreaming the same dream again. I'll be patient. I'll wake up. Etienne is due to throw aside the curtains any moment now. (*Exits.*)

SIMONE. (*Enters with* CLEMENTINE.) Uncle?

LADY. Not here, my dear.

CLEMENTINE. Corignon?

LADY. Alexandre?

CLEMENTINE. Yes.

LADY. He's to assist your uncle in a vital mission. We've been forgotten for the moment. Be patient—be patient. They'll look for us when we've been missed long enough. (*MUSIC—love song reprise.*)

CLEMENTINE. I didn't know it would be this way.

LADY. Living?

CLEMENTINE. Loving—

(*They sing a reprise of the love song, "Tell Me the Answers," as the scene ends.*)

END OF SCENE ONE

ACT TWO

Scene 2

IDENTITY SONG

Is he who he claims to be,
Or isn't he the one who says he isn't who he was
Or wasn't he the one who said
She was who she claims to be
Or wasn't she the one she said she was?

PETIPON. I am Lucien Petipon.
ETIENNE. He is Doctor Petipon.
MONGICOURT. I am Doctor Mongicourt.
MADAME PETIPON. He is Doctor Mongicourt. I am Madame Petipon.
GENERAL. She is Madame Mongicourt.
MONGICOURT. She is Madame Petipon.
ETIENNE. She is indeed Madame Petipon.
PETIPON. She is Madame Petipon.
MADAME PETIPON. I am Madame Petipon.
GENERAL. She is Madame Mongicourt.
ETIENNE. She is Madame Mongicourt.
PETIPON. She is Madame Mongicourt.
GENERAL. As I said, Madame Mongicourt.
MONGICOURT. As he said, Madame Mongicourt.
GENERAL. I am General Petipon de la Grele.
LADY. He is General Petipon de la Grele.
MONGICOURT. She is The Lady. . . .
LADY. I am Madame Petipon.
ETIENNE. She is Madame Petipon.
GENERAL. She is Madame Petipon.
MADAME PETIPON. I am Madame Petipon.
ETIENNE. She is, she is, she is Petipon—Madame.
LADY. I am Madame Petipon.
MADAME PETIPON. Yes, you are Madame Petipon.
CORIGNON. She is Madame Petipon.

LADY. I am Madame Petipon.
MADAME PETIPON. You are Madame General Petipon.
PETIPON. She is Madame Petipon.
MADAME PETIPON. She is Madame Petipon.
GENERAL. As I said, Madame Petipon. His wife.
CORIGNON. I am Lieutenant Corignon.
MADAME PETIPON. He is Lieutenant Corignon.
GENERAL. He is indeed Corignon.
LADY. He is Chou-chou.
ETIENNE. Chou-chou?
CORIGNON. Chou-chou to very special friends.
LADY. Friend.
CORIGNON. Chou-chou to very special—a very special friend.
GENERAL. He is Lieutenant Corignon.
CORIGNON. I am Lieutenant Corignon.
GENERAL. Engaged to my dear niece . . .
LADY. Clementine. Engaged to General Petipon's niece, Clementine.
CORIGNON. I am Chou-chou.
LADY. You were Chou-chou.
ETIENNE. He is Lieutenant Corignon.
LADY. That's all he is.
GENERAL. Lieutenant Corignon.
ETIENNE. I am Etienne. A faithful servant.
PETIPON. Loyal and true.
MADAME PETIPON. Etienne.
MONGICOURT. Etienne.
GENERAL. Etienne.
LADY. ETIENNE.
CORIGNON. He is Etienne.
ETIENNE. Loyal and true.
MADAME PETIPON. I am Madame Petipon.
LADY. You were Madame Petipon.
CORIGNON. She is The Lady. . . .
PETIPON. She was The Lady. . . .
LADY. I am Madame Petipon.
PETIPON. I am Doctor Mongicourt.

ETIENNE. He is Doctor Mongicourt.

MONGICOURT. I am Dr. Petipon.

(*MUSIC as they leave until* MADAME PETIPON *enters and sits.*)

MADAME PETIPON. I simply do not understand my husband, Dr. Lucien Petipon. He is a strange and complex man. I arrive at Touraine to represent our family only to find him there having preceded me by a number of hours. He does not acknowledge me—treats me liked a stranger and stands by while I am insulted. It is altogether strange and perplexing.

(MADAME PETIPON *exits* D. L. *As she exits,* ETIENNE *enters, followed by the* DUKE OF VALMONTE D. R.)

ETIENNE. Madame instructed me as she arrived a moment ago that she was not in to callers. She is quite drawn, haggard, pale, overwrought—in short, her usual self. (*Goes out* U. L.)

DUKE. Tell her that the Duke of Valmonte is here. She will quite understand. How can he describe that angel as drawn, haggard, pale and overwrought? Why, Madame Petipon is—is—

ETIENNE. (*Returns.*) Out to everyone.

DUKE. Madame is fascinating. That is the word, the one word capable of describing her . . . fascinating.

ETIENNE. He's mad. Quite mad.

DUKE. What did you say?

ETIENNE. Too bad. Too bad. It's too bad madame won't receive you.

(DUKE *hands him coins.* ETIENNE *exits.*)

DUKE. I am moved. Quite moved. I am moved. It never occurred to me that a Valmonte could admit to such ecstasy. I am moved, quite moved. I am moved.

DUKE'S SONG: ("I AM MOVED")

I am moved,
I am moved,
I am moved to the roots of my being,
    to the point of not hearing
        or seeing
    any sight that is not my beloved,
        my beloved,
        my beloved.

I am torn,
I am torn,
I am torn and exquisitely shaken.
    Who can tell what this pang
        will awaken
    in a heart never given to passion,
        unto passion,
        unto passion?

It is now,
It is now,
It is now that my life takes a turning
    and my soul feels its first
        bitter yearning
    for a creature who must be an angel.
        oh, an angel,
        yes, an angel.

Can she know,
Can she know,
Can she know I am hers for the taking
    of a chance for romance
        in the making?
My noblesse will oblige me to tell her,
        to tell her,
        to tell her.

It is now that I yearn.
She will know I am torn.
I am moved,
I am moved,
I am moved.

DUKE. I wonder what a Valmonte looks like when he is moved. Ah, quite interesting, even impressive. Ah, what is that? A pimple—a pimple disfiguring a Valmonte nose. I am committing excesses. It is the emotion of the moment. I am too impetuous.

MADAME PETIPON. (*Offstage.*) I told you, Etienne, I was at home to no one.

DUKE. It is the aunt—that female—that dragon.

ETIENNE. (*Offstage.*) But, madame, he said it was urgent.

MADAME PETIPON. Oh, very well Monsieur, Le Duc de Valmonte.

DUKE. Madame.

MADAME PETIPON. Did I not meet you only yesterday at General Petipon's chateau?

DUKE. We met indeed. You were with her.

MADAME PETIPON. Ah yes.

DUKE. And is Madame Petipon in good health?

MADAME PETIPON. A trifle fatigued from the journey, but otherwise quite well, thank you.

DUKE. I trust she did not tire herself unduly at the chateau.

MADAME PETIPON. I would say she had a rather trying time.

DUKE. It is—ah—very clement weather for this time of year, is it not?

MADAME PETIPON. Yes, my heliotrope is already in bloom. . . . Why does he speak in the third person like a servant?

DUKE. If madame will permit me . . .

MADAME PETIPON. Oh, thank you, Monsieur Le Duc.

DUKE. Perhaps I had better return when the household is once again in order.

MADAME PETIPON. Monsieur Le Duc. . . .

DUKE. Madame. . . . (*Exits.*)

MADAME PETIPON. Monsieur Le Duc de Valmonte.

PETIPON. What an insistent, tiresome woman. Arrives unexpectedly at my uncle's chateau, insists that she is a guest, insists that she is my wife, slaps my uncle the General, who then slaps poor Mongicourt, challenging him to a duel—all this because she will insist upon visiting when she is not invited. You here? When did you return?

MADAME PETIPON. Only a moment ago. What was that you were muttering to yourself?

PETIPON. I was musing on Mongicourt's duel and the reason for the slap that began the whole thing.

MADAME PETIPON. It was strange. One would think that General Petipon would have challenged you to a duel —not Mongicourt—

PETIPON. How could you? How could you create the whole ugly situation?

MADAME PETIPON. I assure you I didn't think I was overheard when I casually referred to that woman, whom you later identified as your uncle's wife, as that tart from Montmartre.

PETIPON. For shame. For shame. To hold her youth and beauty against her.

MADAME PETIPON. I simply didn't hear or, if I heard, believe the General when he introduced her to me as Madame Petipon.

PETIPON. What other Madame Petipon could he have meant? You should have paid closer attention—or—which would have been preferable—you should have remained here in Paris.

(ETIENNE *enters with a small bouquet of flowers and a letter.*)

ETIENNE. Flowers and a letter from the Duc de Valmonte. (PETIPON *holds his hand out.*) For madame!

MADAME PETIPON. Give it to me—it's addressed to me. (ETIENNE *surrenders the letter to* MADAME PETIPON, *exits* D. R.) But how extraordinary! Why would he write a letter of this sort to me? All I said to him—the only words that passed between us at Touraine—was my question, "Which, monsieur, is the way to the buffet?"

PETIPON. Let me see. (*She surrenders the letter to him. He hands her the bouquet.*) Unbelievable! "My fortune is yours." "Forget the doctor. Flee with me to London." No encouragement? No encouragement? These letters are not written without some provocation.

MADAME PETIPON. I asked directions to the cold buffet. Mark that—"cold buffet."

PETIPON. You have laid waste to my honor and the sensibilities of the Duke of Valmonte. This could lead to yet another—

MADAME PETIPON. Duel?

PETIPON. Duel! (*Takes the bouquet from her.*) You may well be the death of me and of Mongicourt. Go to your room, my dear, and pray to your many patron saints. (*She exits as* MONGICOURT *enters* D. R.)

MONGICOURT. He was jesting. Surely he was jesting.

PETIPON. The duke's madly in love with her.

MONGICOURT. I mean your uncle and his challenge.

PETIPON. The honor of a general—and a Petipon is no trivial matter.

MONGICOURT. You'll represent me?

PETIPON. My uncle wouldn't understand. He may well want me to be *his* second.

MONGICOURT. But all this is the result of my helping you and pretending that Madame Petipon was Madame Mongicourt.

PETIPON. Ah yes, my dear Mongicourt.

MONGICOURT. Oh.

PETIPON. And that took friendship and personal courage and I thank you. No matter what happens I shall remember your generosity, your selflessness. If necessary I shall have your brave deeds engraved on your tombstone.

MONGICOURT. How can I thank you for such moving sentiments?

PETIPON. I hate to desert you at this crucial moment in your life—but madame and I leave tonight for Italy.

MONGICOURT. Italy?

PETIPON. That is what I wrote to the General this morning. In an hour I shall receive a telegram summoning me to Rome for a consultation on the Holy Father's state of health.

MONGICOURT. Who will deliver the message? One of your wife's apparitions?

PETIPON. Etienne will deliver the message.

MONGICOURT. How do you know all this?

PETIPON. It's my device to avoid the General until everything cools off and your fate and future are decided one way or another.

MONGICOURT. Why the Holy Father?

PETIPON. He's a prisoner of the Vatican—I'd have to go to him—he couldn't come here.

MONGICOURT. But you are playing games with my life.

PETIPON. It's so petty, so minor.

MONGICOURT. My life?

PETIPON. The tiny nick my uncle will give you with his blade. A scratch and pouf!—your hide is safe and his honor satisfied.

(*From offstage we hear the* GENERAL'S *voice.*)

GENERAL. Where is he? Where is he?
ETIENNE. This way, General Petipon. This way.
GENERAL. Where is my nephew?

(PETIPON *and* MONGICOURT *exit* D. L., *as the* GENERAL *enters with* LADY *and* ETIENNE, D. R.)

LADY. I'm not sure Dr. Petipon will be pleased to see me.

GENERAL. Not sure? He'd damned well *better* be

pleased. Put these swords somewhere safe. Fetch him. Now, my dear. Conceal yourself here—until this quarrel is patched up.

LADY. You are a treasure.

GENERAL. (*Leads her to sleeping alcove.*) You are the treasure. (*As* LADY *exits.* MADAME PETIPON *enters* U. L.)

MADAME PETIPON. You!

GENERAL. You!

MADAME PETIPON. We seemed destined to meet.

GENERAL. And in the most unlikely places.

MADAME PETIPON. I beg your pardon.

GENERAL. I have not forgotten your reflection on Madame Petipon.

MADAME PETIPON. An unfortunate slip of the tongue—

GENERAL. For which your husband may well pay with his life.

MADAME PETIPON. You would challenge your own nephew?

GENERAL. As far as I can determine, Dr. Mongicourt is no relative of mine. However, I did slap your husband.

MADAME PETIPON. He said nothing of this to me.

GENERAL. It is not the sort of thing men boast about. (*Walks to table on* R. *as* DR. PETIPON *enters* L. *with bag.*)

MADAME PETIPON. (*Crosses to* PETIPON D. L.) Lucien, your uncle said that he slapped you. You didn't tell me.

PETIPON. I was quite small at the time.

MADAME PETIPON. He seemed to indicate that the offense was committed yesterday.

PETIPON. That was with affection. Just as a pinch can be a sign of love. (*Pinches her cheeks.*)

(*The* GENERAL *chuckles,* MADAME PETIPON *exits* D. L.)

GENERAL. You seem to have a fondness for the ripe ones.

PETIPON. Ripe ones?

GENERAL. You must admit that she's perhaps even beyond ripeness. Gone to seed. Lucien, are you ready to forgive? To forget?

PETIPON. Yes. No. What are you talking about?

GENERAL. Your anger yesterday. The scene you made when you misinterpreted the relationship of your wife and Lt. Corignon.

PETIPON. It's none of my business.

GENERAL. Lucien, listen to an old man— I mean a man older than you. Forgive, forget—

PETIPON. But you haven't received my letter!

GENERAL. Letter?

PETIPON. I wrote to you this morning. The great news. I have forgiven her and we leave tonight for a second honeymoon in Italy.

GENERAL. She'll be delighted.

PETIPON. Who will be delighted?

GENERAL. Your wife.

(LADY *enters from the alcove.*)

LADY. Lucien.

PETIPON. What are you doing here?

GENERAL. Embrace, embrace—seal this sacred moment with a kiss.

LADY. My dear— (*Holds out her arms.*)

(PETIPON *takes* LADY *in his arms and face to face as if kissing they hiss at each other as he walks her* D. L. *as if to force her from the house.*)

PETIPON. Get out.

LADY. No.

PETIPON. Leave.

LADY. I stay.

PETIPON. I don't want you here.

LADY. I'll scream.

PETIPON. Only once. And for the last time.

LADY. You wouldn't dare.

PETIPON. I'll kill you.

LADY. I think you mean it.

PETIPON. I know I mean it.

GENERAL. Children. Children. Save the ardor for Italy.

LADY. He's delighted.

PETIPON. Come with me, dear. (*Attempts to walk* LADY *to the* D. R. *exit.*)

GENERAL. Lucien, one moment. (*Throws the cloth from the chair. Frozen in a zany position of repose is the* STREET CLEANER.)

PETIPON. What in the world?

GENERAL. Very lifelike.

PETIPON. Don't touch him.

GENERAL. Why not?

PETIPON. Paint's not dry yet.

GENERAL. He's hideously real.

LADY. He looks like a street cleaner to me. But that face is familiar— (*Stands beside chair.*) Exactly where did you find—? (*Touches the street cleaner's arm and freezes in place.*)

GENERAL. She's entranced. Off in another world of her own. What an unpractial creature!

own. What an unpredictable creature!

ETIENNE. (*Enters.*) Dr. Petipon?

PETIPON. Yes?

ETIENNE. Two gentlemen to see you. They come as representatives of Lt. Corignon.

GENERAL. They're here.

PETIPON. Who is here?

GENERAL. Lt. Corignon's seconds. Have you forgotten your duel?

PETIPON. I thought he had.

GENERAL. Oh, now that he is to become a member of the family he regrets having challenged you.

PETIPON. I accept his regrets and the duel is off.

GENERAL. You medical men! No. The duel is not off. Show them in. There is still the small matter of honor to be satisfied.

PETIPON. But I'm genuinely fond of the lieutenant.

GENERAL. And, I assure you, he of you. Here, take this! (*Thrusts a sword at* PETIPON.)

PETIPON. What have I done to you?

GENERAL. Nothing! I'm doing you a favor.

PETIPON. By slicing me into bits?

GENERAL. By instructing you as to the use of weapons and the proper handling en garde thereof.

PETIPON. I was always a slow learner at school. Couldn't we put the duel off a few months—years—decades—until I've mastered the art?

GENERAL. By God, I'm glad I was the only person to hear that dastardly remark. Anyone else would have termed you a coward.

PETIPON. I am. I am a coward. Hear me, world—Lucien Petipon is a coward—through and through—and thoroughly proud of it!

(MADAME PETIPON *runs in and is almost impaled on the* GENERAL'S *sword*.)

MADAME PETIPON. Spare him. Spare Dr. Petipon. You know not what you do! (MADAME PETIPON *has retreated around the room. She is suddenly beside* LADY.) Madame! Madame? A proud woman pleads with you for her husband's life. Madame? Urge him to be merciful. (MADAME PETIPON *takes* LADY'S *arm and freezes in place*.)

GENERAL. Will you leave us, madame? You have quite disconcerted Madame Petipon. Madame? Do you hear me? (*Touches* MADAME PETIPON *just as* PETIPON *shouts*.)

PETIPON. No! Don't touch her, Uncle! Even the slightest—— (*Has pointed finger at* GENERAL *in admonishment and the slight touch freezes him in place as well*.)

ETIENNE. (*Enters*.) Dr. Petipon? Have you forgotten the gentlemen in the foyer? They seem most anxious to—— (*Has touched* PETIPON.)

(*We now have a frozen diagonal consisting of the* STREET CLEANER *in the chair*, LADY, MADAME PETIPON, *the*

GENERAL, PETIPON, *and* ETIENNE. *The* SECONDS
enter from D. R. *They are a* PARISH PRIEST *and his*
YOUNG ASSISTANT.)

PRIEST. Blessings on this house. Ah, here you are. And
frozen with amazement, I see, at the sight of a simple
parish priest—announcing that he is to serve as a second
in a private duel—or even public duel for that matter—
either way, it is truly unusual. But we deviate. We deviate. Why am I here to serve as a second in such a
barbaric, savage, encounter known as a duel?
        JULIAN. Because of Lt. Corignon.
        PRIEST. Lt. Corignon? Oh, yes, quite right, quite right.
The dear couple—the precious lambs—God's own. Lt.
Corignon, although pure at heart was forced to confess in
the solemnity of the occasion of the nuptial Mass that
you, madame—yes, you—thank God that you still blush
—you, madame, had been his, Lt. Corignon's, mistress.
        JULIAN. The story was out—
        PRIEST. —and had to be handled discreetly— So the
dear boy begged me to protect you, General, dear Clementine, and in a way you, madame, (*This to* LADY.) by
asking us, Brother Julian and me to serve as his seconds.
        JULIAN. They're too shocked to reply.
        PRIEST. Oh, be not so aghast! Who amongst us have
not been transgressors! He—or she—who is without sin
is invited to cast the first stone. No reaction? I thought
not! (*Goes to* ETIENNE.) Note, how even this lowly servant is moved— I must comfort him, Brother Julian, I
must— (*Touches* ETIENNE *and is frozen.*)
        JULIAN. Father, what is wrong? Are you so overcome
with emotion? Father— (*Touches* PRIEST *and now we
have a line consisting of* STREET CLEANER, LADY, MADAME
PETIPON, GENERAL, PETIPON, ETIENNE, PRIEST, AND
BROTHER JULIAN. MONGICOURT *enters from* D. R.)
        MONGICOURT. (*As he enters.*) My dear Petipon, don't
you think this whole matter can be resolved— (*Sees the*
GROUP.) My God. Mass paralysis! Oh—that chair, that

chair— (*To* PRIEST.) the devil's plaything—as you would undoubtedly say. What a precious event! Dear Petipon— unprincipled and a coward—Madame Petipon—a pious bore—but you, my lovely jewel, my enigmatic lady, why couldn't you give your heart to a fiery, passionate man like me? Ah well, she'll never know. She'll never know. Her loss— (*Plays with the left-hand switch. The* GROUP *whips around as if a current of electricity has passed through them.*) Perhaps the other way. (*A jolt and another violent reaction.*) Ah, it's the other one that turns it off. (*At this moment from each of the remaining three entrances the men involved in the two duels enter. They all enter at the same moment and speak at the same time.* MONGICOURT *enters from* D. R., *the* GENERAL *from the bedroom alcove, the two* PRIESTS *from* D. L.) See here, Petipon.

GENERAL. Niece! Niece!

PRIEST. Ah, General, here I am to do my Christian duty.

CORIGNON. (*Enters from* D. L.) General Petipon, I must inform you—

PETIPON. Lt. Corignon, perhaps you should know—

MONGICOURT. So we meet face to face—the murderer and his innocent victim—

GENERAL. Marvelous, quite marvelous—all parties are ill met by sunlight. Everything can now be resolved in a matter of seconds.

PETIPON. Resolved?

GENERAL. With the ladies out of the way, we can straighten out once and for all the details of our various duels.

PRIEST. Please explain to me, once more, who is to duel with who—

JULIAN. Whom!

PRIEST. And whom is to represent who?

JULIAN. What?

PRIEST. Whom!

GENERAL. Lt. Corignon has challenged Dr. Petipon—

thus Dr. Petipon has the choice of weapons. At the moment he has but one second, Dr. Mongicourt.

PETIPON. Dr. Mongicourt has been challenged by my uncle, General Petipon. Therefore he has the choice of weapons, and at the moment no seconds.

GENERAL. Since our time is limited, allow me to resolve the delicate matter of seconds. Acting for Lt. Corignon, the good Father and his assistant. Representing my nephew, myself and his dear friend, Dr. Mongicourt. And myself.

MONGICOURT. I am honored.

GENERAL. I am proud to serve beside you.

PETIPON. And of your duel, dear uncle?

GENERAL. The Duke de Valmonte and Lt. Corignon will second me.

MONGICOURT. You'll stand up for me, Petipon?

PETIPON. Honor demands that I not turn against my uncle.

GENERAL. Then who is left to represent Dr. Mongicourt?

CLEANER. (*Crawls out from beneath tablecloth.*) It so happens that I am free this afternoon—

MONGICOURT. I didn't ask you to volunteer.

GENERAL. Shame, shame—the man is acting out of the goodness of his heart.

MONGICOURT. The duel is off.

CLEANER. You refuse my offer of assistance?

MONGICOURT. On the contrary, you are acceptable as a witness but I need two— And since my good friend and professional associate, Dr. Petipon, turns his back upon me in my hour of need—I am left with no alternative but to refuse to duel unless adequately represented.

GENERAL. Bravo! (*Calls.*) Etienne, Etienne— (*To* PETIPON.) Allow me the liberty of naming your servant! Etienne!

ETIENNE. (*Enters from* D. L.) Sir?

GENERAL. Have you ever dueled?

ETIENNE. I?

GENERAL. You!

ETIENNE. Strange as it may seem!

GENERAL. Yes?

ETIENNE. Yes!

GENERAL. You will stand up for Dr. Mongicourt, and choose his sword.

ETIENNE. Pistol!

MONGICOURT. Pistol?

ETIENNE. I have noticed a slight cast to General Petipon's right eye which happens to be his squinting eye for target practice. A pistol therefore would be your safest and wisest choice of weapons. He will be able to see you and hit you only by the greatest of mathematical odds. Your chance of hitting him—since your eyesight seems remarkably unaffected by your years—is mathematically to your advantage.

GENERAL. In Africa we beat clever servants to death.

ETIENNE. And in Paris there are those who try to starve us to death. Dr. Petipon—I am relieved to say—is an exception to the rule.

PETIPON. Scalpel!

GENERAL. Scalpel?

CORIGNON. Scalpel?

PRIEST. Scapular?

PETIPON. Scalpel!

CLEANER. Scalpel?

DUKE. Scalpel?

MONGICOURT. Scalpel?

PETIPON. Scalpel!

MONGICOURT. Marvelous!

PETIPON. Why not?

GENERAL. Why not?

PETIPON. A sword is a natural weapon for Lt. Corignon to use—consider his profession.

MONGICOURT. And considering Dr. Petipon's profession what could be more appropriate than a—

CORIGNON. Scalpel?

PETIPON. Scalpel!

CORIGNON. Mon général?

GENERAL. He does have choice of weapons and while it may seem cruel—even inappropriate—there is, you must admit, a certain je ne sais quoi to the selection. Scalpels—

CLEANER. At how many paces?

MADAME PETIPON. (*Enters* U. L., *followed by* LADY.) Paces?

CLEANER. A term derived from the ancient French art of dueling. Dueling until sufficient blood is let to the satisfaction of the offended party.

MADAME PETIPON. Are we talking metaphorically, theoretically, or literally?

GENERAL. Alas, madame, the last. As this erudite gentleman has stated your husband dies today—his honor intact and my honor satisfied.

MADAME PETIPON. (*Runs to* PETIPON.) I will die with you. My voices have told me that our fates are inseparable.

GENERAL. Shame, madame, shame—

MADAME PETIPON. Shame?

GENERAL. To throw yourself into your lover's arms before the very eyes of his wife—and your husband.

MONGICOURT. I think we, for once and for all, ought to clear up this misapprehension—

PETIPON. You should challenge me to a duel, Uncle.

GENERAL. I?

PETIPON. I owe you an apology and a death— Madame Mongicourt is, in reality, Madame Petipon— (*Then indicating* LADY.) And Madame Petipon is—is—

LADY. —at liberty.

DUKE. Then I may speak? I may kneel before you?

LADY. If that's your pleasure.

GENERAL. I have been deceived!

MADAME PETIPON. I have been betrayed!

PETIPON. I know! Betrayed by me!

MADAME PETIPON. No—by him!

DUKE. By me, Madame Petipon?

MADAME PETIPON. He knows my name! Mark how clearly he pronounced—Petipon!

DUKE. How have I betrayed you?

MADAME PETIPON. You wrote to me . . . proposing that I run off with you—

DUKE. But that was a mistake—

MADAME PETIPON. The only mistake you made was to spurn me. (*To* PETIPON.) Honor demands that I now accept his proposal.

GENERAL. The honor of this entire assembly has been jeopardized because of one man. One man has placed us all in this acutely embarrassing position.

PETIPON. Who is that?

MONGICOURT. You ask?

PETIPON. I ask—

LADY. It's true—

PETIPON. What's true—

MONGICOURT. We are the victims of one man's egotism.

PETIPON. And who is that man?

MADAME PETIPON. You dare ask?

PETIPON. I dare ask— Who is that man?

ALL. You dare ask?

(CLEMENTINE *enters from* D. L.)

CLEMENTINE. Father— Uncle, Uncle, forgive me, I couldn't stay in Touraine any longer. I had to be with Alexandre.

CORIGNON. Clementine!

GENERAL. Clementine!

MADAME PETIPON. Clementine.

PRIEST. Dear child, wandering about Paris, alone, unchaperoned— I won't allow myself even to contemplate what Fate might have in store for you.

LADY. There she is, another cruel victim of brutal men and their selfishness. The Duke de Valmonte being of course an exception. And you, mon général, another.

CLEMENTINE. I don't understand.

PRIEST. There are times when the heart needs no explanation.

CORIGNON. You must trust me, Clementine. You must allow me the sacred privilege of being the keeper of your trust.

LADY. The brute. The very words, the very words—

GENERAL. She is overcome with grief—

DUKE. I will comfort her. . . .

GENERAL. I will comfort her. . . .

LADY. You both may comfort me!

CLEANER. I haven't got all day. What about the duels?

GENERAL. Off—both are off—

CLEANER. That's an arbitrary decision.

GENERAL. Not at all—we have a conflict of honors here and at such moments one does not duel. I would say that all was forgiven but not forgotten.

LADY. I would perhaps be willing to forget at Maxim's. (*Starts to leave.*) Will you join me, monsieur le Duc?

DUKE. I will!

LADY. And you, mon général?

GENERAL. I will!

PETIPON. The two of them?

LADY. You learned so little from our brief marriage. Two may be company—but three is a triangle—with many possibilities. (*SONG.*)

IDENTITY SONG REPRISE

Is he who he claims to be,
Or isn't he the one who says he isn't who he was
Or wasn't he the one who said
She was who she claims to be
Or wasn't she the one she said she was?

(LADY *exits with the* GENERAL *and the* DUKE *as the Act ends. LIGHTS UP on exactly the same pose as the curtain. Song for curtain call. Perhaps material similar to opening of the Act.*)

PROPERTY PLOT

On Stage:
    Sheet
    Newspapers
    Lone flower
    Dress
      (Also Petipon's jacket with glasses and wallet with
        francs)

Stage Left:
    Tray with teacup
    Small suitcase with letter
    Knitting square
    Medical bag
    Bell
    Shawl

Stage Right:
    String bag with lemons
    Dress box
    Riding crop
    Armchair with gloves
    Broom
    Two package bundles
    Cane
    Two bouquets—one with note
    Swords in towel
    Prayerbooks—two
    Priest's censer
    Hatbox—mail
    Single rose
    Pearls
    Books for girls
    Party hat
    Rx pad, money for tip
    Pocket watch
    Will
    Handkerchief
    Card

Cloth
Knife and fork
Card
Coin
Mirror
Sheet
Napkin
Bouquet of daisies